CHRISTOPHER THE OGRE COLOGRE, IT'S OVER!

by Rebeldita the Fearless and Dr. Siu

From the *Rebeldita the Fearless* series by Dr. Siu

Design and llustrations: Víctor Zúñiga

Translation: Matthew Byrne

Christopher the Ogre Cologre, It's Over!

1st Edition
© Oriel María Siu 2021
www.orielmariasiu.com

Design and Illustrations: Víctor Zúñiga
www.victorgrafico.com
Translation: Matthew Byrne
www.matthewdbyrne.com

ISBN: 978-0-578-92409-0

To Berta Cáceres and to all children in occupied lands — for truth.

More than 500 years ago, across the wide Ocean A
there lived a king and a queen, so greedy were they.
EuroLandia is what their home was called - right by the sea -
Oh, they hoarded everything there, as far as the eye could see!

Rivers and land, and gold shore to shore,
mountains and cows, yet they wanted much more!
"This is not half enough!" they'd huff and they'd hum,
and they wouldn't be happy 'til they owned every last crumb.

To take and to take, each day more and more,
they had one hundred Ogres to steal and explore.
With their big huge arms, they'd hoard everything.
These Ogres snatched birds flying free with the wind.

And just as expected, the day finally arrived
when those greedy kings' well ran completely dry.
No more land or animals left for them to take -
not even a flake of old yucky fruitcake!

But then a thought occurred to those wicked kings,
"Why don't we just go steal other people's things?!
To faraway lands, that's where our Ogres must go!
Why we're just thinking of this? We simply dunno!"

And to head this big job, the kings would now choose
their most trusty Ogre, so they asked themselves, "Who?"
But the answer was easy, a minute it took.
They knew just the Ogre who would make history books!

"We've made our decision," the evil kings roared,
"He's the biggest, the baddest, by all Ogres adored!
He's ambitious and malicious - just totally vicious!
Ruthless and heartless, and savagely capricious!
Christopher Cologre, we Kings do choose you!
There just isn't an Ogre that steals like you do!"

"Go to faraway lands,
and bring us more gold.
We want more of everything:
land, clouds, birds, LOTS MORE!
We know they've got riches and treasure galore,
so in the name of our Lord, we choose YOU to explore!"

The Ogre Cologre in the blink of an eye,
set sail for new land - didn't even ask why.
He always craved stardom - and this was his chance.
"I'll be faaaamous!" he shrieked, with a song and a dance.

And with one hundred Ogres, Cologre sailed Ocean A.
So much sea - 'twas so grueling - that he barfed all the way!

Until FINALLY - one day in October - they could not believe their eyes!
What a surprise it was, they had reached PARADISE!
Beautiful clouds, mountains so grand,
jewelry, gold, architecture well-planned.

Majestic big jaguars,
and birds in the sky,
full markets and rivers,
what beauty, Oh My!

There, millions of children ran free like the breeze
playing so happy, right next to the sea.

Cologre blinked twice, his eyes opened wide,
"My eyes must be tricking me - they're going side to side!
I just can't believe it, could this be all true?
I'd rather not think it! I've got work to do!"

"I'll steal and I'll steal until I can't anymore.
I'll be *faaaamous,*" he screeched, "You will not ignore!"

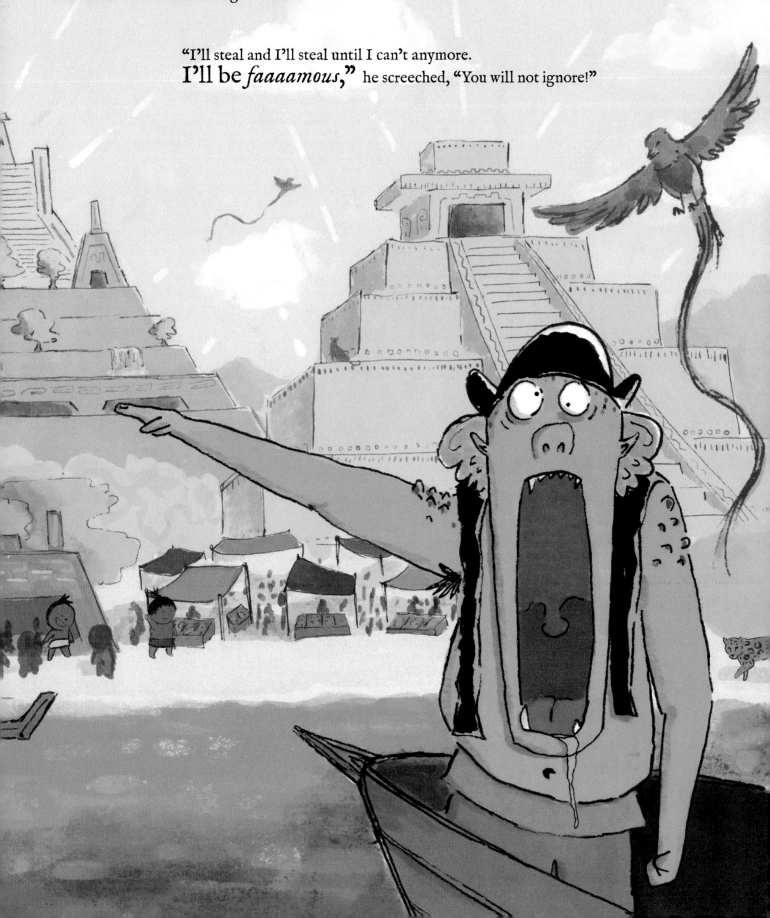

The Ogre Cologre read his first OgreCommand
and began to speak with a swish of his hand:

1
prohibit you
telling
the truth

" From
this
moment
on, you'll
do as
I say!

Get used to it kids, 'cause I'm here to stay.
You'll all work for me, and you'll do it for free,
you'll bow to my ways - this is how things will now be.
Give me all of your gold, your mountains, your cakes!
Your clouds and your books and ALL of your lakes!
Everything here by decree is now mine.
My kings handpicked ME, so it's MY time to shine!"

"And listen you AbyaYalans, and heed my advice
or you'll be quite sorry - I won't say it twice!
You must learn my language and worship my kings
because henceforth, I pull ALL of the strings!

"I'm Christopher the Ogre Cologre, I'll be famous one day.
They'll say I was GREAT in every which way!
I'll make books say I was perfect - even my ugliest tooth,
'cause from here on out, I PROHIBIT YOU TELLING THE TRUTH!

"I need to make sure that from each pair of lips
comes only a great story of my three big ships.
Anyone who dare call me an Ogre instead
will regret it when I scream, "Off with his head!"

The children and parents of AbyaYala were steaming
"If you think we'll obey,
YOU MUST BE DAY DREAMING!!!!!"

And to defend MotherEarth,
they knew what was right.
So the children put up the greatest of fights.
They didn't want Ogres stealing their land,
but Ogres were mean and chose to expand.

Oh, and how sad the scene was...

Cologre's crew
brought
guns,
rifles
and sickness.
Children and parents
now suffered great
illness.

Millions of AbyaYalans
fell to the ground,
and the emptiness made
the most saddening sound...
of loss.

But those awful Ogres,
they felt no remorse
about what they did
- a pure show of force.

Now we can see how Cologre began
to loot AbyaYala - his original plan.
His dastardly Ogres had all come prepared
to take all they could - nothing was spared.

They put jaguars and mountains with all of the gold
in dirty great ships
to later be sold.
They looted the rivers and took every bird,
they burnt all their great books,
'twas completely absurd!

(I give you my word. I'm honest and true.
Believe what I say - unlike you-know-who.)

Ogres took children's smiles,
their grandparents' styles,
the breeze of the sea,
and the birds over water, like the wind, flying free.

Truth be told, SO much beauty AbyaYala had to its name
that Cologre decided he needed more arms to lay claim.   And so, he yelled:

"Bring me more people, more girls and more boys!
And FORCE them to work FOR ME at my employ!"

And Cologre's Ogres went in no time
to where they committed another unforgivable crime...

AfricaTheBeautiful was the name of the land,
for it, another horrible fate, the Ogres had planned.
From there to AbyaYala, they took children in big ugly ships
held captive in chains 'round all of their hips...

Such was how,
despite the children's bravery,
      these Ogres put millions of them
      in slavery!

This story of Cologre has not often been heard,
but I'm telling the truth - this really occurred.

If you've never heard it - please do not despair;
it's 'cause Christopher Cologre made truth something you couldn't declare.
He made sure every book would spread these tall tales:
That the greatest admiral he was, an explorer who sails
the great ocean blue, and from Genoa hails.

So, over the years, people came to believe:
he "discovered" new land - millions he deceived.
They thought of him brave - "he had such derring-do" -
they called him "bold" and "super smart," too.

'Twas all a big lie - he was none of these things!
Sorry, Cologre! *The truth sometimes stings!*

("Discovering" a place? What a *DOOFUS* he was!
You know what they say: silly is as silly does.
100 **million** people in AbyaYala already existed
- over thousands of years they had beautifully persisted!)

It's been 'bout 500 years since that day in mid-Fall
when Cologre usurped AbyaYala once and for all.
And though the Ogre Cologre isn't around anymore,
his fibs and his lies remain like before.

But listen dear children
because in this story I tell
wonderful things DO happen as well!

Well back then, in May,
while Cologre looked away,
a wise bean-eating grandma did something bold you could say!
She climbed the highest mountain many believed was uncrossable.
This amazing grandma, oh she sure did the impossible!

"I ate lots of beans for my power and might,"
this *abuelita* laughed in total delight.
"That Ogre Cologre won't find us up here.
If we stick together, we'll be in the clear!"

She took seven children and puppies with her
to that lush and green mountain, oh so happy they were!
A Big Ceiba covered them, and so they bravely climbed,
feeling safe in that refuge, paying Ogres no mind.

Inside little caves, they laid out their cots
and grew their own food on fertile dirt plots:
yucca and plantain, in rows two by two,
and corn of all colors, from yellow to blue.
Tomato, avocado, and chocolate, too!

They planted beans and legumes in patches yards-long.
This nourishing food meant they'd all grow strong.

Chickens visited, too, and hens that laid
the most exquisite eggs - Triple A Grade!

All the while, the children NEVER forgot
to share fair-and-square, as Cologre had not.
In this mountain, happiness shone like a sparkling jewel,
'cause together they fought Cologre's cruel rule.

Every night, when the sun went down,
the children set off in a group towards town.
Following maps they had carefully made,
to Ogreland they went, on quiet crusades,
to bring children their freedom, which Cologre forbade.

They walked and they ran under cover of night.
The moon and the stars lent them all of their light.
They crossed the Ogres' plantations on paths unpaved
to free all the children Cologre enslaved.

And when they'd arrive, they whispered real low:

"Wake up! Wake up! There's no time for sleeping.
We're getting you out, but the Ogres are creeping.
We have to act fast for our plan to take shape
'cause the night is short, and you have to escape!"

Well would you believe it?
Rescue after rescue, their numbers grew large.
They called this RESISTANCE, with *abuelita* in charge!

There were no longer seven
or even ten or eleven.
Now there were hundreds
of children in *abuelita's* safe haven!

And in this one mountain
they made fires galore.
They danced without fear
and spoke their languages once more.

Because every morning, as the sun shone bright,
the *abuelita* - an old woman now, losing her sight -
shared stories with them to their great delight.

About AfricaTheBeautiful so they'd never forget,
and honor AbyaYala as their destinies met.
She spoke of where they came from, where their roots reside,
and the catchy cool songs they carry deep inside.
This *abuelita* taught them dances with pride
and the immense knowledge the ancestors provide.

This superb grandma her knowledge she shared,
everything she knew of this world - no one compared.

But life can be tricky, it doesn't always go right.
When fighting the good fight, things aren't always so bright.

One day, on accident, the children let slip
a delicious smell that made Cologre's mouth drip!
It was the smell of the *abuelita* deliciously cooking,
and after that wonderful aroma the Ogres came looking!

And when the Ogres came running over the hill,
the *abuelita's* heart began to grow ill...

"Pum pum!" it sounded
"PUM PUM!" her heart pounded.
So the *abuelita* called them, and soon they all surrounded:

"Listen to me children,
listen all the way through,
I don't know how much more time I'll be here with you.
So, in case anything happens,
there's ONE THING you must do:

OUR HISTORY, you must WRITE IT.

Do not let Cologre steal the truth from us, too!"

Cologre got furious, yelling, **"she'll pay the price!"**
just as *abuelita* finished giving her advice...

But Cologre was too late! Before he could do harm,
the children banded together and sounded the alarm!
A gigantic smile soon appeared on each mouth
'cause the ace up their sleeve
was rumbling down south...

A STIIIIIIIIINKYYYYYYY,
MOST POTENT
and *DEAAAAAADLY*
FART
the children unleashed!

And what a FOUL odor -
'twas not a loud cough,
it was more like a bomb
that had just gone off!!!

The children had stuffed themselves
with soft yummy beans
to be at the ready,
like farting machines!

And just as the children had carefully planned
'twas a fart no Ogre could ever withstand!
Away Ogres ran screaming like chickens and hens,
never to return or be heard from again.

But...
with lots of kisses
and a tear in each eye,
the children bid the *abuelita* a bitter goodbye.

Oh, but you best believe they followed her advice
'cause they got down to writing without thinking it twice.

The children soon put together a most fantastical book
with Ceiba tree bark – just give it a look!
Under firefly flicker, writing felt right
'cause as if by magic, their words just took flight!

They then placed their book very deep inside
the big Ceiba tree as a safe place to hide.
"So that one day," the children agreed,
"someone frees AbyaYala from Cologre's lies
and land-grabbing greed."

But MANY years passed and no one arrived
to look at their book - yet their hope survived.

Tired they grew, however, of waiting so long,
and as they got old, their hope grew faint
like the sound of a gong.

And during that time, more Ogres arrived
to poor AbyaYala, which barely survived.
The Ogres raised up gigantic huge walls
and divided the land, yet no one recalls.

And Christopher Cologre? He died over there
in a EuroLand town - without much fanfare.
Yet though he is gone, he remains to this day
a "hero" to many - to my great dismay.
The lies that he told and the yarns that he spun
are still told as truth - they've not been undone.

SO much time passed,
days turned into years -
and we fast approached
today it appears!

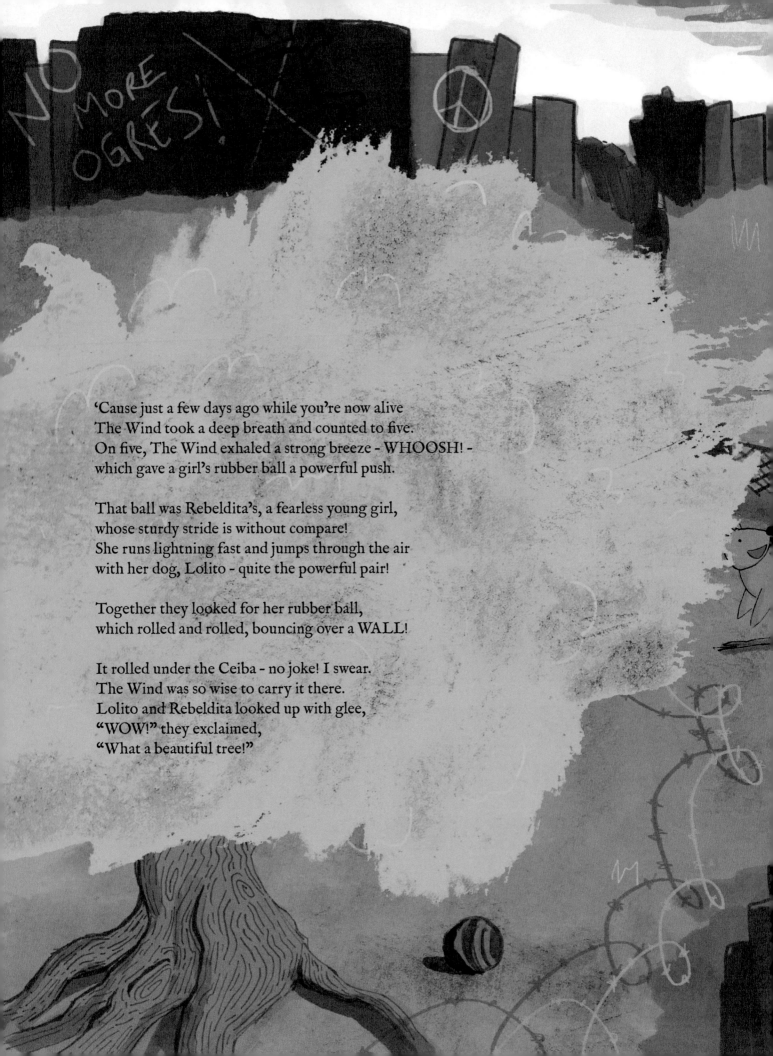

'Cause just a few days ago while you're now alive
The Wind took a deep breath and counted to five.
On five, The Wind exhaled a strong breeze - WHOOSH! -
which gave a girl's rubber ball a powerful push.

That ball was Rebeldita's, a fearless young girl,
whose sturdy stride is without compare!
She runs lightning fast and jumps through the air
with her dog, Lolito - quite the powerful pair!

Together they looked for her rubber ball,
which rolled and rolled, bouncing over a WALL!

It rolled under the Ceiba - no joke! I swear.
The Wind was so wise to carry it there.
Lolito and Rebeldita looked up with glee,
"WOW!" they exclaimed,
"What a beautiful tree!"

She reached for the ball.
Something caught her off guard:
a shiny, green leaf - its brightness unscarred.

She took a quick peek,
and a branch brushed her cheek,
then the Ceiba, suddenly,
to Rebeldita began to speak:

"Rebeldita," the tree whispered,
"I have something for you,
deep in my hollow, kept safe out of view.
You're fearless, I know,
and we need your help now
for truth to be known,
only you will know how."

"What's this?..." Rebeldita reached inside
and when she got it out, "A BOOK!" the Ceiba replied!
So, you best believe, Rebeldita opened it wide.

"WOOOOOOOOW - it's so pretty!
The coolest of letters in beautiful twists?
This, I know, I just cannot resist!"

She took a deep breath
and started to read.
And *each word so transformed her*
that she felt herself *freed*.

From this great book she had in her hand,
she learned she lived on occupied lands.
"I'm Black and Beautiful,
Native and Grand!"
she learned, too,
plus words that allowed her
mind to expand:

"Our Existence is Resistance!" the
prohibited book read,
and in her heart Rebeldita felt these magic
words spread.

She also learned the true name of the land she lives on,
(not the name the Ogres gave it, on maps they had drawn);

"Ab-ya-Ya-la," pronounced Rebeldita
      "Ab-ya-Ya-la," she whispered out loud,

            "Ab-ya-Ya-la," she yelled, incredibly proud.

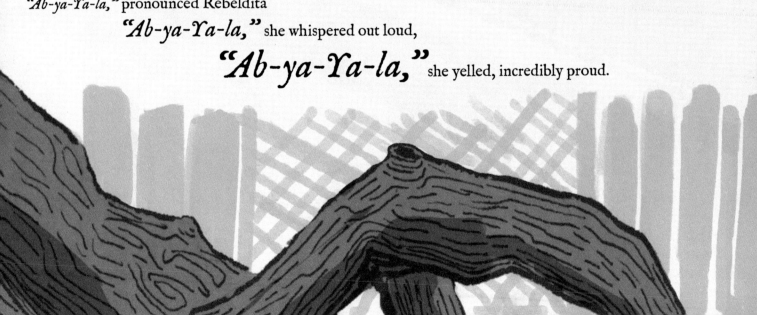

She read every inch of the book, cover to cover.
It had troves of knowledge for her to uncover!
So much, in fact, she had to share with you -
that history needed to be rewritten anew.

So Rebeldita decided to take a pen in her hand
and write her own book - the one in your hands!

Because she knows
that you'd
do your best
to
honor the truth
and lay Cologre's lies forever to rest.

EVERYWHERE - North, South, East, or West!
As AbyaYalans, your ancestors request:
that you do it for them,
that you do it for you,
that you guard the truth whatever your quest!

'Cause there's still some time to love and embrace
and make this world a more beautiful place.

So go!

Go free AbyaYala from Ogre lies
no matter what their tricky disguise.

'Cause *nobody can deny you
your history* and right
to control your future
and make it shine bright!

(There's a happy ending
in this book, you see,
you've got the truth now.
    You can now be free.)

And if you're *reeeeeeeeal* quiet
you'll be able to hear
the children's laughter,
    rejoicing in glee.